-8444

Daniel's Mystery Egg

Alma Flor Ada

Illustrated by
G. Brian Karas

Green Light Readers
Harcourt, Inc.
Orlando   Austin   New York   San Diego   London

4/2013

Daniel found a surprise.
It was a small white egg.
He put it in a little box.

Daniel ran to tell Alex. "Look! This is the best egg ever! What could it be?"

"Maybe it will be an ostrich with a long neck!" said Alex.

"You can take it to school for
show-and-tell. I can help you."

"I won't need help," said Daniel.
"I think a small animal will come
out of this egg."

Next, Meg came to look.
"Daniel found this egg," said Alex.
"What could it be?"

"Maybe it will be an alligator
with big teeth!" said Meg.

"Alligators are not good pets. Maybe you will have to move out of your house. You can all move in with me!"

"We won't need to move," said Daniel.
"I think a nice animal will come out
of this egg."

Next, Tammy came to look.
"Daniel found an egg!" said Meg.
"What could it be?"

"Maybe it will be a duck that quacks all the time!" said Tammy.

"Your house will be very noisy. You will have to teach the duck to quack softly. I can help you."

"I don't think the house will be noisy,"
said Daniel. "I think a quiet animal
will come out of this egg."

"Well, Daniel," said Alex, "what will this small, nice, quiet animal be?"
"We'll have to wait and see," said Daniel.

So they waited, and waited,
and waited....

And then…

One day the egg hatched!

"It doesn't have a long neck," said Alex.
"It doesn't have big teeth," said Meg.
"It doesn't have a noisy quack,"
said Tammy.

"No," said Daniel. "But it IS small, nice,
and quiet. It's the best lizard ever!"

Guess the Animal!

**Daniel's lizard was a big surprise.
Write a riddle about another animal.**

1. Think of an animal.

2. Write three clues about it.

3. Trade clues with a friend.

4. Read the clues.

It is green.

It eats bugs.

It is smaller than a book.

5. Try to guess the animal!

Meet the Author and Illustrator

Alma Flor Ada learned to read out in the garden. Her grandmother taught her by writing the names of plants in the dirt. Even now, Alma Flor Ada's favorite place to read and write is outdoors. Many of her stories are about animals and nature.

Alma F Ada

G. Brian Karas used to live in Arizona. There he saw lots of lizards like Daniel's. Brian made the pictures for this story in an interesting way. First he glued bits of colored paper on white paper. Then he painted pictures on this background. "Sometimes I tear up my old artwork and use it in my collages," he says. "I hope you'll try making and painting collages, too. It's fun!"

G Brian Karas

To Daniel, with hugs and kisses

—Abuelita

For information about permission to reproduce selections from this book,please write to Permissions, Houghton Mifflin Harcourt Publishing Company 215 Park Avenue South, NY NY 10003.

www.hmhbooks.com

First Green Light Readers edition 2001
Green Light Readers is a trademark of Harcourt, Inc., registered in the United States of America and/or other jurisdictions.

The Library of Congress has cataloged an earlier edition as follows:
Ada, Alma Flor.
Daniel's mystery egg/by Alma Flor Ada; illustrated by G. Brian Karas.
p.   cm.
"Green Light Readers."
Summary: When he finds an egg, Daniel and his friends try to guess what is inside.
[1. Eggs—Fiction.]   I. Karas, G. Brian, ill.
II. Title.   III. Green Light reader.
PZ7.A1857Dan 2000
[E]—dc21   00-9728
ISBN 978-0-15-204885-3
ISBN 978-0-15-204845-7 (pb)

SCP 10 9 8
4500396773

Ages 5–7
Grades: 1–2
Guided Reading Level: G–I
Reading Recovery Level: 15–16

Green Light Readers
For the reader who's ready to GO!

"A must-have for any family with a beginning reader."—*Boston Sunday Herald*

"You can't go wrong with adding several copies of these terrific books to your beginning-to-read collection."—*School Library Journal*

"A winner for the beginner."—*Booklist*

Five Tips to Help Your Child Become a Great Reader

1. Get involved. Reading aloud to and with your child is just as important as encouraging your child to read independently.

2. Be curious. Ask questions about what your child is reading.

3. Make reading fun. Allow your child to pick books on subjects that interest her or him.

4. Words are everywhere—not just in books. Practice reading signs, packages, and cereal boxes with your child.

5. Set a good example. Make sure your child sees YOU reading.

Why Green Light Readers Is the Best Series for Your New Reader

- Created exclusively for beginning readers by some of the biggest and brightest names in children's books

- Reinforces the reading skills your child is learning in school

- Encourages children to read—and finish—books by themselves

- Offers extra enrichment through fun, age-appropriate activities unique to each story

- Incorporates characteristics of the Reading Recovery program used by educators

- Developed with Harcourt School Publishers and credentialed educational consultants